SCHOOL BUS

This Book Belongs to:

GOLDEN FREIGHT LINES

JOLLY ROGER

Hop Aboard! Here We Go!

We go by car
     And we go by train,
We go by boat
     And we go by plane.
We go by land
     And sea and air,
We go, go, go,
     From here to there.

GO, GO, GO!

STERLING CHILDREN'S BOOKS
New York

An Imprint of Sterling Publishing
387 Park Avenue South
New York, NY 10016

ISBN 978-1-4027-7222-1 (hardcover)

Published in 2012 by Sterling Publishing Co., Inc.
By arrangement with J B Publishing, Inc. on behalf of the Richard Scarry Corporation
41 River Terrace, New York, New York
This book was originally published in 1967.

Distributed in Canada by Sterling Publishing
c/o Canadian Manda Group, 165 Dufferin Street
Toronto, Ontario, Canada M6K 3H6
Distributed in the United Kingdom by GMC Distribution Services
Castle Place, 166 High Street, Lewes, East Sussex, England BN7 1XU
Distributed in Australia by Capricorn Link (Australia) Pty. Ltd.
P.O. Box 704, Windsor, NSW 2756, Australia

For information about custom editions, special sales, premium and corporate purchases,
please contact Sterling Special Sales Department at 800-805-5489 or specialsales@sterlingpublishing.com.

This edition designed by Neo9 Design, Inc.

Manufactured in China
Lot#:
6 8 10 9 7 5
10/15

www.sterlingpublishing.com/kids

RICHARD SCARRY'S

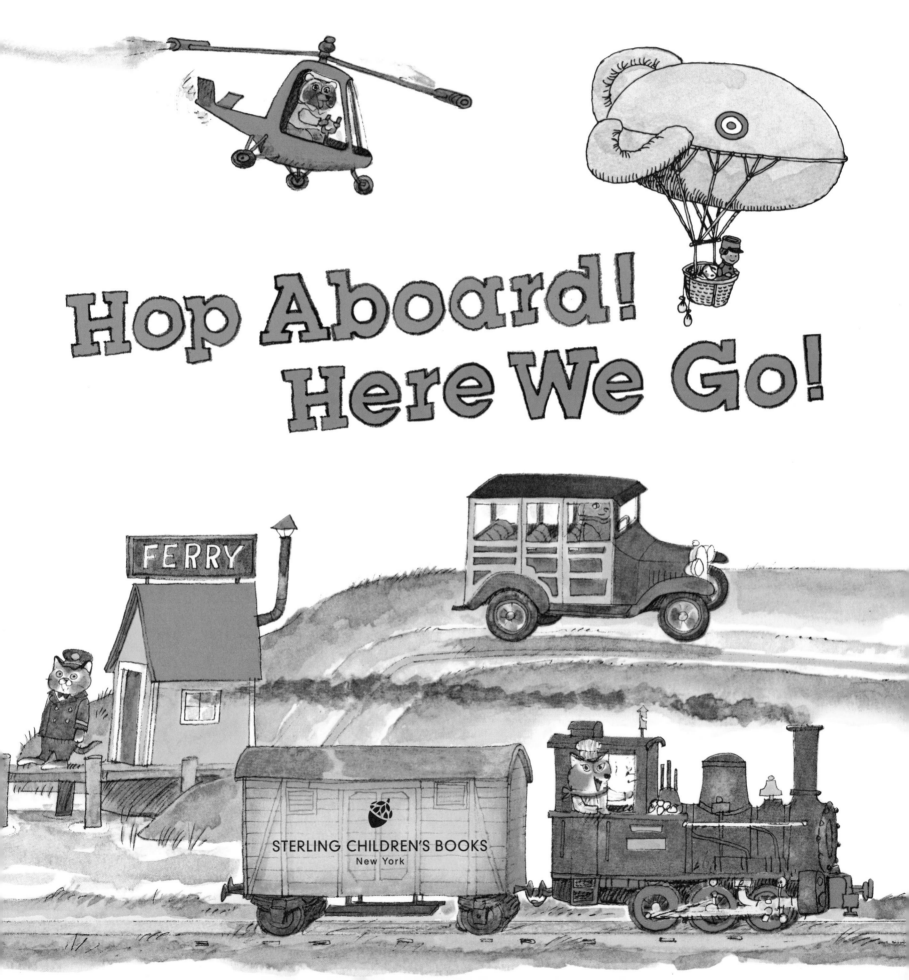

Hop Aboard! Here We Go!

STERLING CHILDREN'S BOOKS
New York

FERRY

Cars,
Buses,
and
Trucks

Here are Roger and Flip, out for a ride in their convertible.

When Flip is in a hurry, he always takes a taxi.

The mail truck delivers the mail.
Do you have a letter for me, Mailman Roger?

Policeman Roger cruises the streets in his patrol car to make sure that there is no trouble.

Would you like to ride in the top of a double-decker bus?
Hop aboard then, and see the sights of the city.

Vrrroooomm!

Roger and Flip roar around
the racetrack in their race car.
I hope they win, don't you?

The delivery motorcycle is
carrying a small package from the
store to the customer's house.

GOLDEN FREIGHT LINES

This big trailer truck is carrying a heavy load of books from the printing plant
to the store. Roger and Flip like to read books when they're not working.

TELEPHONE COMPANY

Roger, the telephone man, is going to put
a new telephone in Flip's house. Do you like
to talk on the telephone?

The garbage truck grumbles and growls,
packing the garbage inside. When it is full,
off it rumbles to the dump.

There's room for lots of friends in Roger's station wagon. You can come, too. Hop aboard!

A pickup truck is handy to have on a farm. "It sure holds a lot of chickens," says Flip.

There's just room for Roger and Flip in this speedy little sports car.

Fire Chief Roger whizzes to fires in his red fire chief's car.

The school bus takes the pupils to school and brings then home again in the afternoon. My, the pupils look wide awake this morning!

The auto carrier delivers new cars to the showroom. Flip has already picked out the car he wants.

The little drugstore car delivers medicine to people's homes, to help them feel better fast.

The concrete mixer's drum grinds around and around, mixing the concrete on the way to the job. What do you think Roger and Flip are going to build with all that concrete?

Cowboy Roger and his sidekick Flip drive their cattle to a greener pasture in the livestock truck.

Whoops! The dump truck tips up, and Flip gets tipped out.

The sturdy jeep can go almost anywhere. Up hill or down, through sand or mud, it never gets stuck.

The big gasoline tanker delivers gas to the filling station.

Here comes the milk truck, delivering bottles of milk.

This truck delivers crates of sodas to stores.

This rescue truck can go on land or water. Silly Flip was swimming too far out, and Roger had to rescue him.

Here comes the ice-cream truck. *What flavor ice cream would you like, Flip?*

The motor scooter goes **put-put-put** down the street. *Hold on tight, Flip!*

The motorcycle policeman chases after speeding cars.

Big buses carry many passengers and all their luggage. Sometimes they go all the way across the country. Flip is taking a cross-country trip for his vacation.

Don't fall off that ladder, Flip!

When a house catches on fire, the brave fire brigade rushes to the rescue, sirens shrieking. Don't worry, they will put out the fire.

The hook-and-ladder is so long that it needs two drivers, one to steer the front and one to steer the back. The firemen use the long ladder to rescue people and to get closer to fires in tall buildings.

Kitty! Get out of that burning house this instant!

The pumper truck pumps water from the hydrant through the long hose.

The ambulance will take anyone who is hurt to the hospital.

This old-time electric taxi ran on batteries. The driver sat in the back.

This truck is used to carry baggage and tired dogs around a railroad station.

Flip and Roger are on an expedition to the South Pole. Their snow tractor's treads crunch over the snow and ice.

ANTARCTIC EXPEDITION

The strong trailer truck carries this heavy power shovel from job to job. I wonder if Flip's getting ready to dig up some old bones?

Old station wagons had sides of beautiful polished wood.

Roger and Flip scoot along in their old-time "Tin Lizzie," enjoying the breeze and the fresh air.

The airport limousine takes pilots and passengers from the city to the airport.

The big logging trailer hauls logs from the forest to the sawmill, where they are cut into boards.

Oh dear, Flip's car has crashed. Roger's tow truck tows the car to the garage for repairs.

The happy children sing "Mary Had a Little Lamb" as the little bus takes them to nursery school.

This old-fashioned car has a rumble seat in the back to carry extra friends.

Flip uses his large, comfortable town car when he is in the big city. "To the circus," he tells his chauffeur.

There go Roger and Flip in their dandy red sports car.

Here comes the big snowplow, clearing snow from the roads and spreading sand on the slippery spots.

The back of the high-lift dump truck rises high up to dump its load. *Look out, Flip!*

People who live in a trailer can take their home along as they travel about the country.

But do you think Flip's little car can pull that big, heavy trailer?

Airplanes,
Helicopters,
and
Rockets

What makes this big zeppelin stay up in the air? It's filled with gas so it can float in the sky.

From their observation balloon, Roger and Flip look down on the earth. If they want to go higher, they just drop a sandbag. *Look out below!*

Early airplanes were made of wood and canvas, and they often had two or more wings.

Some Early Planes

A monoplane was an old-time plane with only one wing.

A plane with three wings was called a triplane.

Here are Roger and Flip looping the loop in a *Spad* biplane, a plane with two wings.

Zzzzooommm!

There go Roger and Flip in a speedy *Albatross*.

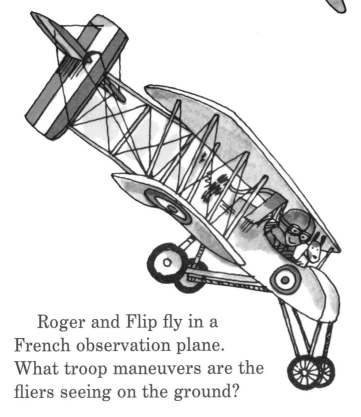

Roger and Flip fly in a French observation plane. What troop maneuvers are the fliers seeing on the ground?

Vrooomm!

There they go again, this time in a *Sopwith Camel*.

The big engines of the B-17 *Flying Fortress* make a deafening roar.

The B-24 *Liberator* rumbles through the sky.

Here come Roger and Flip in a fast little plane called the *Mosquito*.

This plane is a German *Stuka*. It's painted in camouflage colors.

The camouflage on this *Messerschmitt* 109 makes it look like a flying leopard.

This P-38 *Lightning* looks as if it could eat its way through the clouds with those sharp teeth.

Roger and Flip climb high into the sky in their P-51 *Mustang*.

Down dive Roger and Flip in their speedy *Spitfire*.

A small light plane is just right for Roger and Flip.

A helicopter can fly straight up and down as well as forward, so it can land almost anywhere, even on top of a building. This helicopter is taking passengers to the airport to catch a plane.

The *Flying Boxcar* is an enormous freight plane. It can deliver its cargo to faraway places much faster than any truck, train, or ship can.

Research planes test new designs and equipment.
Brave test pilots Roger and Flip are flying this one.

Roger has invented this
strange flying machine for
short hops. Do you think it
will work?

Navy aircraft carrier planes have wings
that fold up when not in use. That way,
many planes can be squeezed together on
the deck of the aircraft carrier.

Some helicopters are so big and
powerful that they can lift heavy trucks.

Astronaut Roy is orbiting the moon in his command module. He's waiting for the lunar module and his astronaut friends to come back from the moon.

The Mercury space capsule carried the first American astronaut into orbit around the earth. Would you like to be an astronaut?

This Gemini Spacecraft carried two astronauts into Earth's orbit.

Roger, Flip, and their friend James are about to land their lunar module on the moon. What will they find there?

Trains and Locomotives

This tiny locomotive was the first steam engine to run along railroad tracks.

The *Tom Thumb* was the first locomotive to run in America. Early locomotives were so slow that Flip could have beaten any of them in a race.

Chugg-chugg, Chugg-chugg

This early locomotive was called *Puffing Billy* because of the way it huffed and puffed along the tracks.

Even though this locomotive was called the *Rocket,* it didn't go much faster than you can run.

Sparks and smoke flew from the *Dewitt Clinton* as it pulled its stagecoach-like carriages along the tracks.

Clang-clang, clang-clang!

Roger rings the *Lafayette's* brass bell as they pull into the station.

This type of steam locomotive pulled passengers and freight cars and helped to settle the American West.

Old-time locomotives were painted brightly. This is one of Roger and Flip's favorites.

Flip wants to drive this locomotive. Do you think Roger should let him?

The docksider is a special engine used to pull freight cars along the docks
of a busy port.

The diesel switch engine
is used in railroad yards to
switch cars from one train
to another.

This is a European steam engine pulling a small boxcar. What do you think is in that boxcar? Flip wishes it were full of dog biscuits.

This is a diesel engine pulling a tank car. What's in it? Is it gasoline or oil? Neither! It's full of good, fresh milk!

This electric locomotive gets its power from the wire overhead. Most of the passengers are sound asleep in the sleeping car, but engineers Roger and Flip are wide awake and alert as their train speeds through the night.

Luggage and mail cars carry luggage and letters from city to city.

Most passengers travel in a coach car.

The passengers have their meals in the dining car. I wonder what's for dinner tonight?

A dome car is a special car that gives the passengers a better view of the scenery.

The diesel locomotive runs on diesel oil. It pulls either freight or passenger trains.

The electric locomotive doesn't give off any smoke, so it
is used around big cities and where there are long tunnels.
Here comes a tunnel now. *Pull in your head, Flip!*

This passenger car has its own motor and is used for short runs.
Engineer Roger sits in the front compartment.

Roger and Flip take their friends up the mountain on the rack railway. The engine's toothed wheel fits into a toothed rail and pulls the train up the mountain.

Flip loves to whiz along above the ground. Would you like to ride on a monorail?

In the city, Roger and Flip take the subway. It rumbles through tunnels underneath the city streets.

Ships
and
Boats

The first boat was probably a raft,
made by tying a bunch of sticks together.
Do you think you could make a raft?

The Phoenicians were among
the earliest great seafaring people.

Ships like this sailed the Nile River
thousands of years ago. They had a sail
to catch the wind and an oar for steering.

Roger, bold Viking prince, sails
the ocean in his Viking ship.

This early Greek warship had a sail and oarsmen, too. The shields
protected the rowers during battle. Flip is the lookout in the forecastle.

Ships with many masts and sails could travel to faraway places. Christopher Columbus sailed the *Santa Maria* from Spain to America.

The Pilgrims sailed to America on the *Mayflower*.

"Yo ho ho," sing the desperate pirates, as they search the high seas for treasure ships to rob.

Whaling ships sailed all over the world, searching for whales. "Thar she blows!" cries Captain Roger. He's spotted one!

Fishing schooners sailed far out to sea to fish for cod and halibut. *Where's your fish, Flip?*

Clipper ships were the fastest and most beautiful sailing ships. They carried cargo to and from ports all over the world.

If you lived in a houseboat, you could float from place to place and always be at home.

Siren screaming, the speedy police boat rushes to help anyone who is in trouble on the water.

"Be careful where you squirt that hose," says Flip.

Aqrrrrooooooo!

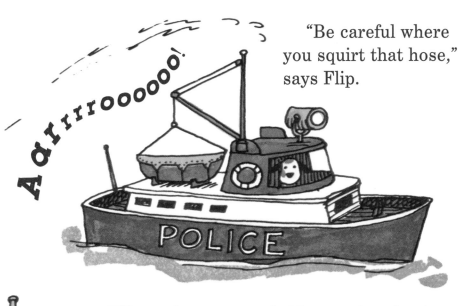

POLICE

Where there are no bridges, a ferryboat carries passengers and cars from one shore to another. This ferry is double-ended, so it doesn't have to turn around as it goes back and forth across the water. *Do you get to steer going back, Flip?*

Fireboats put out fires on other boats and docks.

F.D.

JANE

MARY

A tanker has many tanks for carrying oil. Later, the oil is used to make our cars go.

Cargo ships sail all over the world, taking on cargo in one port and delivering it to another. The cargo might be food or cars or almost anything. How about toys?

A train ferry carries trains across lakes, rivers, and channels. The cars are rolled onto rails in the boat and tied down.

If a boat is in trouble,
it's Roger and Flip to the
rescue, in their trusty
Coast Guard lifeboat.

The aircraft carrier has a wide,
flat deck. Airplanes use it for a
runway, to take off and land.

The patrol torpedo boat, or PT boat, is a small
but very fast warship.

People live on an ocean liner for days as it crosses the ocean.

The hull of the hydrofoil boat rises out of the water as the boat speeds up. When the hull is completely out of the water, the boat can really speed along.

Toot, toot!

STAR

The little tugboat whistles as it pulls the barge upriver. Some tugs help ocean liners to dock. Others push or pull barges. Up and down rivers, and all around the harbor, tugs are busy, day and night.

Roger puts his net over the side of his fishing boat. When he and Flip haul it back in, it will be full of fish—they hope!

Submarines can sail on the surface of the sea, or dive deep down under it. Research subs take scientists deep underwater to study sea life. *What strange deep-sea fish do you see, Flip? Not a sea monster, I hope!*

Some boats are just-for-fun boats. Roger uses his little rowboat to explore the ponds and streams near his house.

A sport fishing boat is used for deep-sea fishing. *Did you catch anything this time, Flip?*

The outboard motorboat speeds over the waves.

The racing boat skims the top of the water. Flip likes to feel the spray on his ears.

This large cabin cruiser has bunks and a kitchen. On long trips, Roger and Flip eat and sleep aboard.